By P. Alanna Roethle
Illustrations by Ed Slocum

Fonts used in this book include:
Tw Cent MT, Cooper Black,
Toyland, and Jokerman

Illustrations were created using an Apple iPad® Pro

Paperback

ISBN-13: 978-0998107707
ISBN-10: 0998107700

In the night, the cool night
As the moon looked down
Rat's eyes shone in the pale light.

"Get out, Rat, get out, you rat"
They said, "Away with you!"
Away he ran before they called the cat.

Rat was too small to say "no"
Too scared to stand up
And they all said he had to go.

He had no time to think of Mom
He forgot about his pile of things
He didn't think about the cat named Tom.

Through the night Rat runs on soundless feet
While the sand is cool
But the silence is not complete.

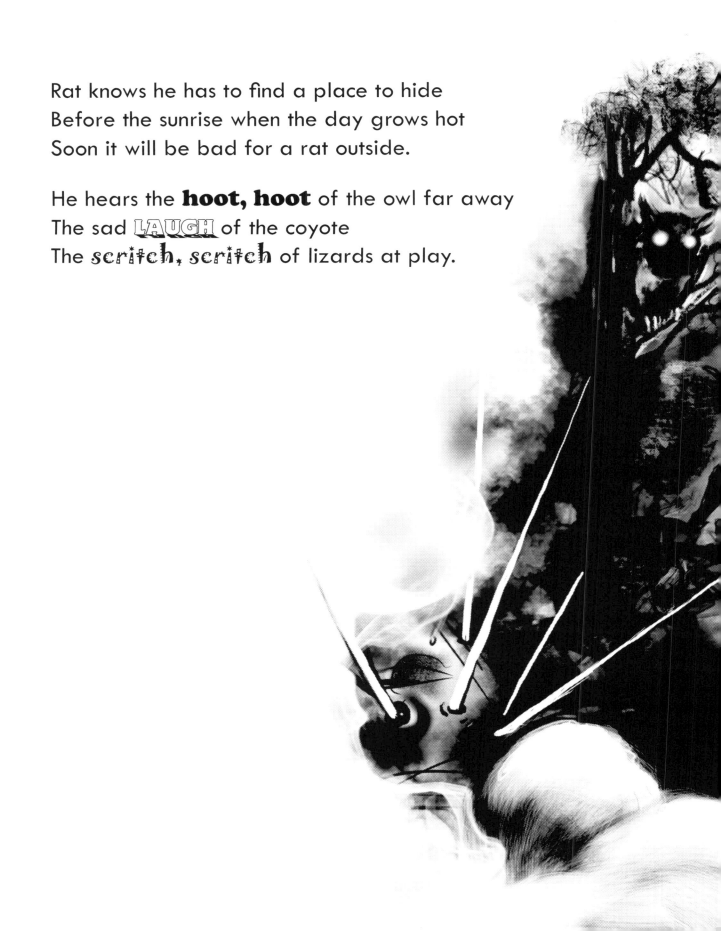

Rat knows he has to find a place to hide
Before the sunrise when the day grows hot
Soon it will be bad for a rat outside.

He hears the **hoot, hoot** of the owl far away
The sad LAUGH of the coyote
The *scritch, scritch* of lizards at play.

The stars watch as the hours pass by
Rat runs, and runs, his breath comes fast
The sky lightens, night sounds begin to die.

A rustle behind him, he doesn't look back
He spies a hole in the rocks
Front feet first, he jumps in the crack.

Rat sleeps, curled in a tight little ball
His whiskers tremble, and his dreams are long.
When he wakes, he sees a great Rat Hall.

He tiptoes through, and begins to explore
Little rat paths move through the dark
Cacti spines surround the door.

Around the bend he smells a feast
Was this all for him?
Enough food for a year, at least.

Before him is the perfect bed
Feathers and grass, warm as can be
"I've got everything I need," he said.

Rat forgets to be lonely, forgets he is small
He runs in a circle, he jumps for glee
He dances and dances - he has it all.

He dashes outside, he forgets to be scared!
He finds a round rock, a shiny bauble
"I'll make a new treasure pile," Rat declares.

His rat sense alerts him, he's full of fright
Something bad is lurking here!
And he freezes — like a thief in the night.

Whisper, rattle, *hiss hiss hiss.*
In the shadows the snake is coiled
Rat doesn't know if he'll escape this.

He bolts away, he's filled with dread
Rat runs so fast his feet are blurs
The snake strikes with his diamond head.

Mr. Snake takes a big bite of pain
Cactus in his mouth looking like teeth!
On the mountains above it begins to rain.

Snake slides away with his new cactus grill
But Rat doesn't have time to be relieved
A flash flood pours down the canyons and the hill.

Water rises from the arroyo
Rat climbs up quick and watches the storm
From above on the arm of a saguaro.

He takes a deep breath of the desert smell
Like concrete, dirt and fresh-cut grass
The day is washed clean and all is well.

The sun peeks out and paints the sky
Cicadas BUZZ and blooms open wide
The angry clouds blow right on by.

As the flood dries up and puddles leave messes
Rat sees the castle walls below
There must be a king nearby, he guesses.

There's no one here but Rat alone
Standing tall above it all
Looking down at his castle home.

Things aren't always what they seem
Look around and you might see
You're already in the place you dreamed.

In the night, the cool night.
As the moon looks down
Rat's eyes shine with a new light.

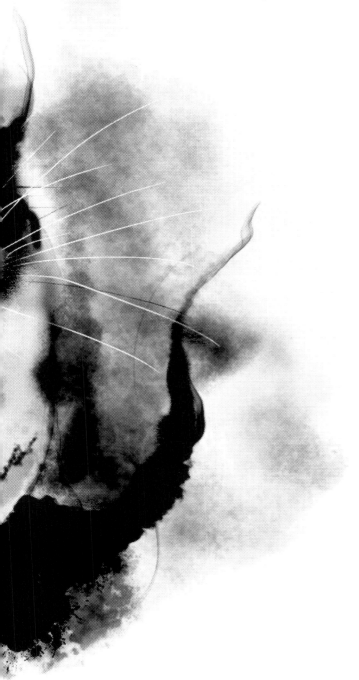

Behind his walls, his safe walls
Lives a great King Rat
In the peace of the desert where the night falls.

AND RAT LIVED HAPPILY EVER AFTER

THE END

Neotoma devia is the Latin name of the pack rat, wood rat, or trading rat that is found only in the Sonoran Desert of far western Arizona. They love bright, shiny objects and will collect them (which is where they get their "pack rat" or "trading rat" name). Pack rats live in nests often made of cactus spines, and Mr. Snake finds these nests very difficult to enter. Sometimes pack rats become a bother, if they decide to nest in vehicle engine compartments or chew on electrical wires.